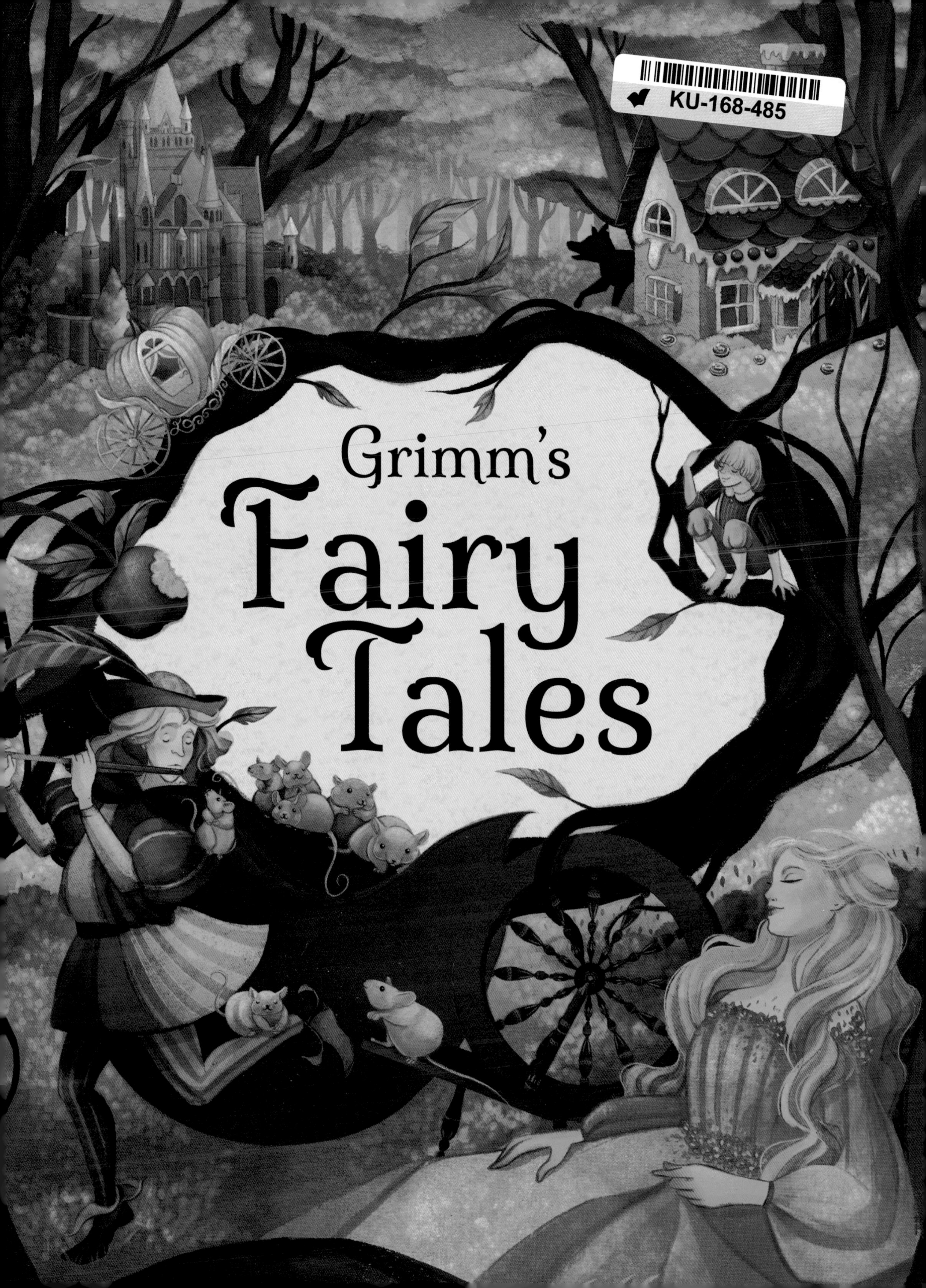
Grimm's
Fairy
Tales

Grimm's Fairy Tales

ARCTURUS

This edition published in 2019 by Arcturus Publishing Limited
26/27 Bickels Yard, 151–153 Bermondsey Street,
London SE1 3HA, UK

Cover Illustration: Alessandra Fusi

ISBN: 978-1-78950-926-7
CH001863NT
Supplier 29, Date 0819, Print run 9085

Printed in China

Contents

The Pied Piper of Hamelin

ONCE UPON A TIME, A LONG TIME AGO, THERE WAS a small town in Germany called Hamelin. It was a prosperous town full of rich merchants and wealthy traders. The people wanted for nothing. Their granaries were full of corn, and their cellars had the biggest barrels of wine in the region. Life in Hamelin was good.

Then, one day, a terrible calamity struck the town. A big black rat appeared. It had a pointed muzzle and red eyes. At first, the inhabitants did not pay much attention to it. But then, a second rat arrived, then a third, then a fourth! Within a few days, the town was overrun by thousands of rats. The streets, squares, and even the houses were swarming with the nasty creatures. And these rats were not afraid of anything.

They fought the dogs, bit the horses, attacked the cats, and when people tried to chase them away with a broom or a shovel, they came back moments later in even greater numbers.

The situation was becoming intolerable. The inhabitants were getting more and more worried, so they decided to call a meeting in the town hall square to try and find a solution.

"This can't go on," one of them said. "The rats are eating up everything. Soon, we won't have anything left in our winter stores!"

"Before the rats came, Hamelin was a clean, quiet town. Look at the state these creatures have thrown us into," added another.

"We must drive out the rats as quickly as possible. This has gone on for too long," they all shouted together.

The crowd was becoming more and more restless. In order to calm them down, the mayor of Hamelin came out of the town hall and addressed them.

"Dear fellow citizens, we are going through a difficult time. But I am sure that, in the end, these rats will leave the town."

"Well, just what are you going to do to get rid of them?" demanded the unhappy people.

"I'm going to call together my statesmen to come to a decision," he replied.

But the inhabitants of Hamelin had already waited too long, and they demanded an immediate solution. The mayor took out a big purse from his pocket and said the first thing that came into his head: "Here is a purse full of gold. I am prepared to give it to the person who will get rid of the rats for us."

A great silence fell on the town hall square. People were busy thinking about what they could do with a purse full of gold. But none of the inhabitants of Hamelin actually knew how to get rid of the rats. Just then, a voice was raised from the middle of the crowd.

"I—the Pied Piper—am prepared to take on the job." Everybody looked with astonishment at the one who had just spoken. It was the first time he had been seen in the town. Tall and slender, the man had strange, piercing eyes and a long, very thin moustache. He wore strange clothes, too, and he held a flute between his fingers.

"Can you get rid of all the rats in the town for us?" asked the mayor, amazed.

"Certainly. And I guarantee that they won't come back," said the stranger.

The townsfolk of Hamelin were dumbfounded. The mayor himself did not know what to think.

"Well, since you know what to do, get to work! What are you waiting for?" he said.

"First, we must settle one last detail. That purse full of gold seems but poor payment to me. I demand a gold piece for each rat that leaves the town," said the Pied Piper.

A murmur ran through the crowd.

"A gold piece for each rat!" cried the mayor. "But that's impossible! There must be several hundred or even several thousand rats in Hamelin!"

"There are a million of them," said the Pied Piper calmly. "And I will not work for less than a million gold pieces."

"I need to think this over. I will call together my statesmen ... It is an enormous sum of money that you are asking for!"

"I give you till tomorrow morning," replied the Piper with a smile.

The mayor summoned his statesmen urgently.

"This man is our last hope. But paying him a gold piece for each rat seems an awful lot to me," he told them.

"We shall have to put up the taxes. The people will become discontented and choose another mayor," said one of the statesmen anxiously.

"But wait a minute, who's talking about paying him?" cried the mayor. "We can easily accept his proposal, let him do his work, and then drive him out of the town afterward without paying him anything."

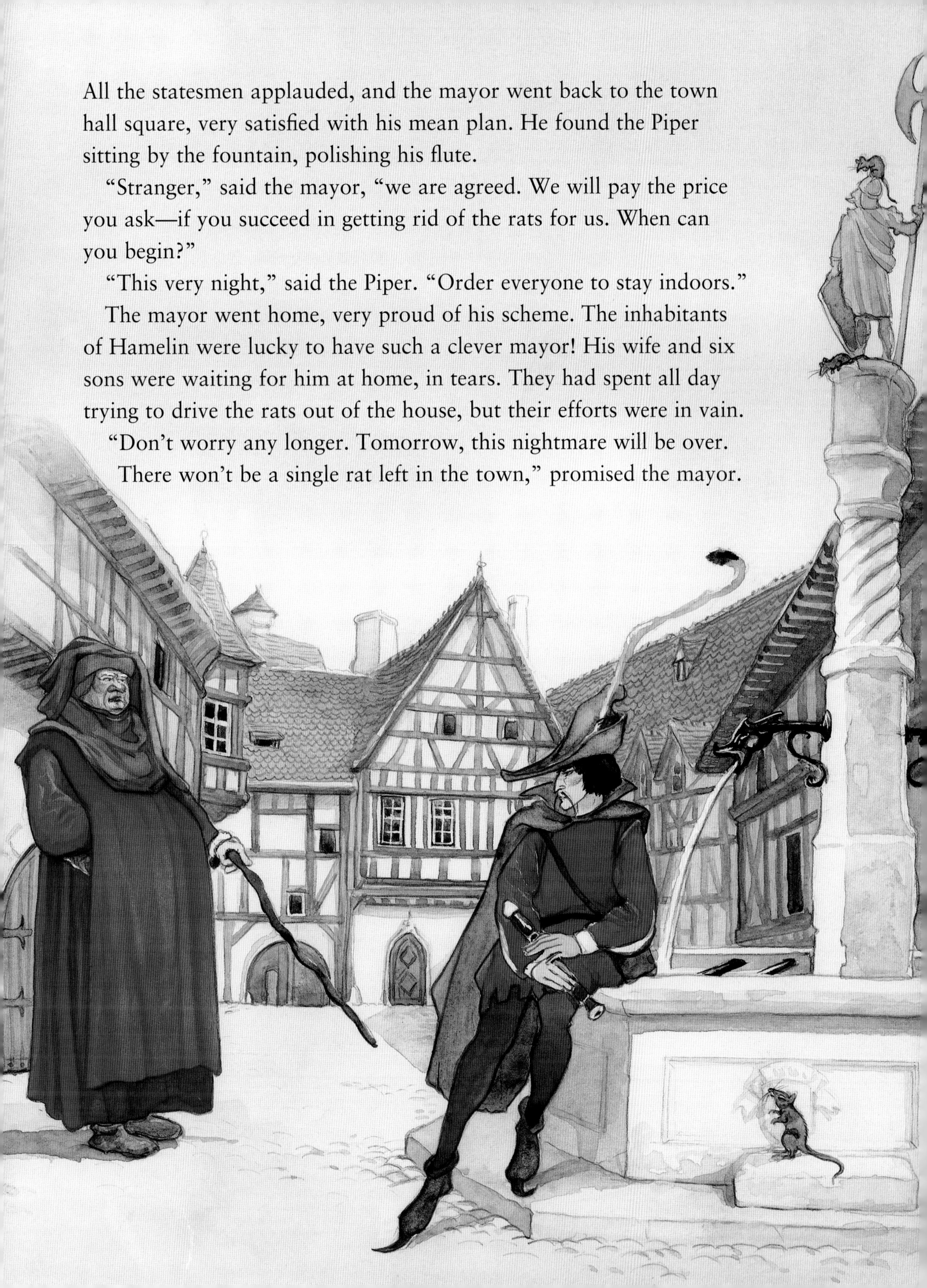

All the statesmen applauded, and the mayor went back to the town hall square, very satisfied with his mean plan. He found the Piper sitting by the fountain, polishing his flute.

"Stranger," said the mayor, "we are agreed. We will pay the price you ask—if you succeed in getting rid of the rats for us. When can you begin?"

"This very night," said the Piper. "Order everyone to stay indoors."

The mayor went home, very proud of his scheme. The inhabitants of Hamelin were lucky to have such a clever mayor! His wife and six sons were waiting for him at home, in tears. They had spent all day trying to drive the rats out of the house, but their efforts were in vain.

"Don't worry any longer. Tomorrow, this nightmare will be over. There won't be a single rat left in the town," promised the mayor.

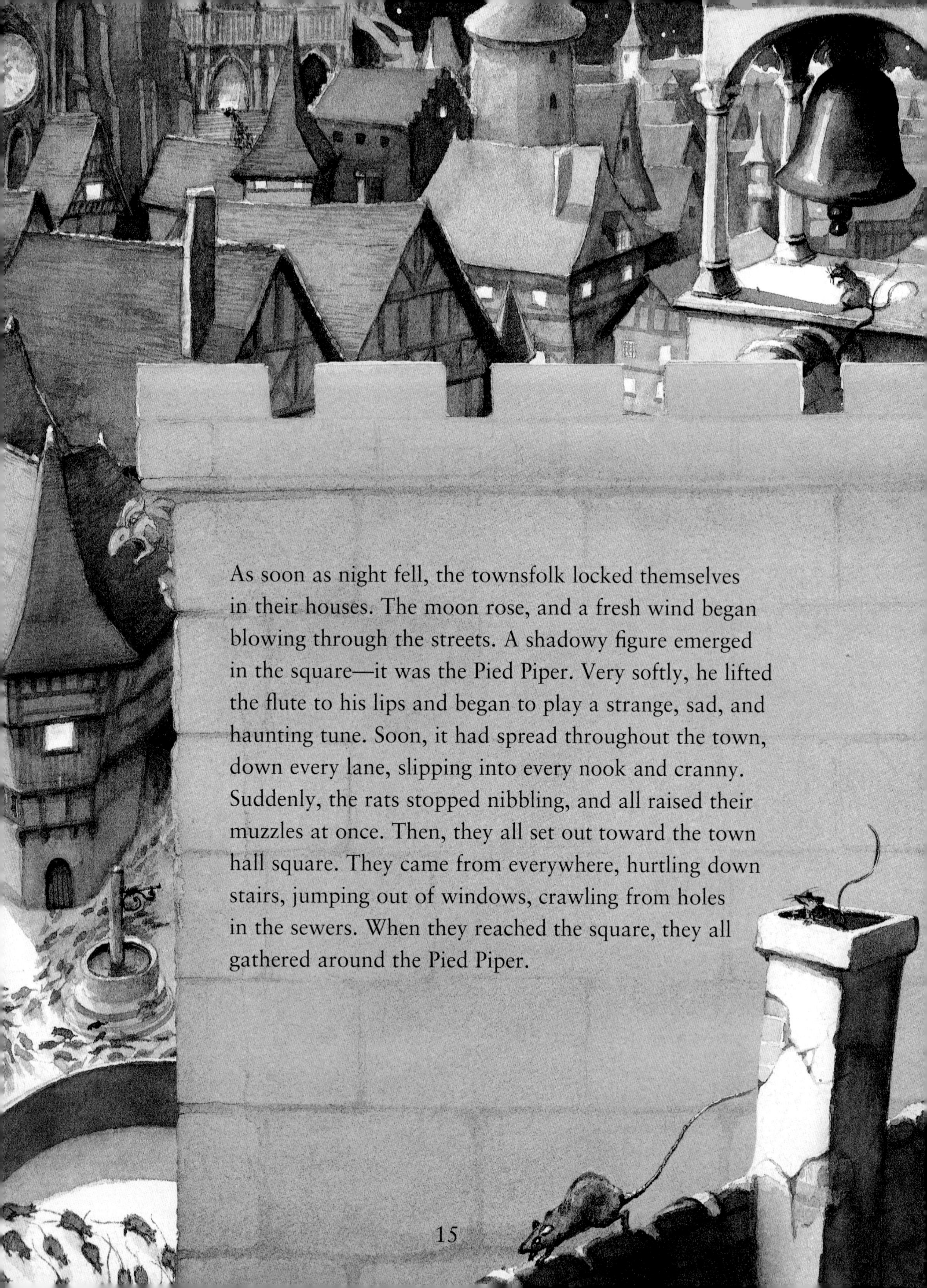

As soon as night fell, the townsfolk locked themselves in their houses. The moon rose, and a fresh wind began blowing through the streets. A shadowy figure emerged in the square—it was the Pied Piper. Very softly, he lifted the flute to his lips and began to play a strange, sad, and haunting tune. Soon, it had spread throughout the town, down every lane, slipping into every nook and cranny. Suddenly, the rats stopped nibbling, and all raised their muzzles at once. Then, they all set out toward the town hall square. They came from everywhere, hurtling down stairs, jumping out of windows, crawling from holes in the sewers. When they reached the square, they all gathered around the Pied Piper.

Very slowly,
the Piper
began walking
toward the town gates, playing
his flute all the while. Noiselessly, the
throng of rats followed him, as if hypnotized.

From their windows, the inhabitants of Hamelin watched the creatures flood past, and they, too, were struck dumb with amazement.

The Piper walked to the Weser River, which ran outside the town. He stopped at the water's edge and looked at the mass of rats spread out before him, every one of them staring at him with beady eyes. Suddenly, he commanded them: "Jump!"

And without hesitating a moment, all the rats flung themselves into the freezing water and disappeared, one after another. When not a single rat was left on the bank, the Pied Piper stopped and went back into the town. The night was dark, and all the inhabitants were asleep.

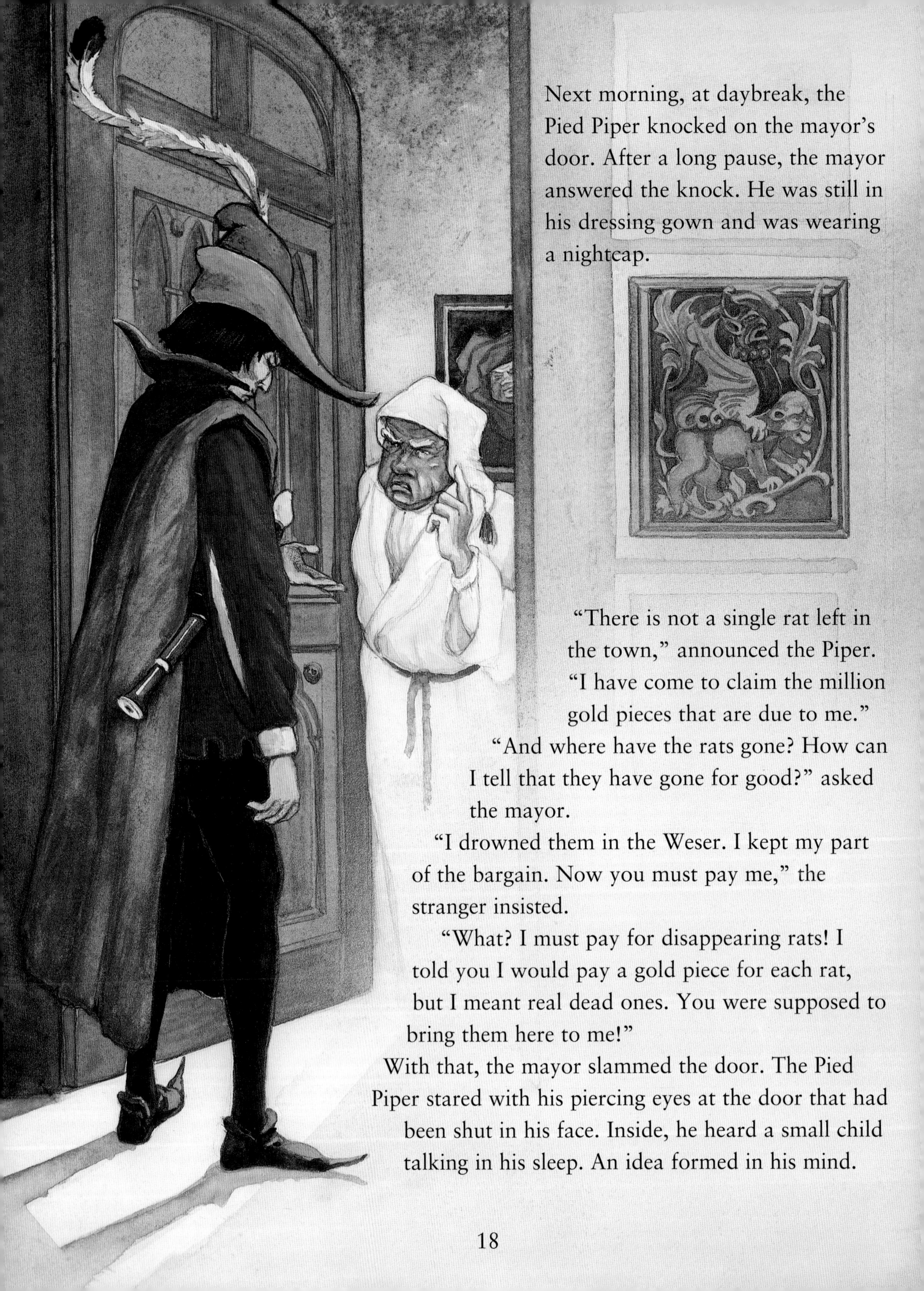

Next morning, at daybreak, the Pied Piper knocked on the mayor's door. After a long pause, the mayor answered the knock. He was still in his dressing gown and was wearing a nightcap.

"There is not a single rat left in the town," announced the Piper. "I have come to claim the million gold pieces that are due to me."

"And where have the rats gone? How can I tell that they have gone for good?" asked the mayor.

"I drowned them in the Weser. I kept my part of the bargain. Now you must pay me," the stranger insisted.

"What? I must pay for disappearing rats! I told you I would pay a gold piece for each rat, but I meant real dead ones. You were supposed to bring them here to me!"

With that, the mayor slammed the door. The Pied Piper stared with his piercing eyes at the door that had been shut in his face. Inside, he heard a small child talking in his sleep. An idea formed in his mind.

"I will surely find a way of making them pay for my services," he muttered. And he turned on his heel and walked away.

A little later, the mayor, in very good spirits, went to the town hall and summoned all the inhabitants of Hamelin to the square. When everyone had arrived, he spoke.

"Dear fellow citizens, I have rid Hamelin of the scourge that had fallen upon it. Today, there is not a single rat left in the town! To celebrate this success, I invite you all to a great banquet tonight at the town hall."

That evening, the people of Hamelin got ready to attend the mayor's banquet. They put their children to bed and went off to the town hall. There, they drank, ate, and danced all through the night. Meanwhile, the Pied Piper wandered alone through the town streets.

The moon rose, and a fresh little wind began blowing. The Piper lifted his flute to his lips and began to play a merry, lively tune that spread even to the darkest and most forgotten alleyways. Suddenly, house doors opened ...

... and the children poured out to gather around the Pied Piper. Then, he began walking toward the town gates, playing all the while. The children followed, smiling and humming. They did not take their eyes off him, just as if they had been hypnotized. Soon, the Piper came to the Weser River. He crossed the bridge with all the children and began climbing the mountain on the other side. Still, the children followed him and did not seem to feel at all tired. The bigger ones carried the smaller ones, and they were all laughing and dancing together. Soon, every one of them had disappeared into the night.

Early next morning, when the inhabitants of Hamelin returned home from the town hall, they searched in vain for their children. The mayor of Hamelin ran through all the rooms of his house, desperately calling for his six sons, but they were gone. Then, he found a piece of paper nailed to his door, on which was written: "Received on account for the disappearance of one million rats: 253 children from the town of Hamelin."

It was signed "The Pied Piper."

The mayor became wild with distress. The children of Hamelin were never seen again, but even today, on misty evenings, when the moon rises and a fresh little wind begins to blow, far off on the mountain, you can hear a strange tune played on a flute and the echo of children's laughter. From that day on, the mayor of Hamelin always kept all his promises, down to the last detail.

THE END

Hansel and Gretel

ONCE UPON A TIME, LONG AGO, THERE WAS AN unfortunate woodcutter who lived with his family in a little house built of wood and thatch, at the edge of a great, enchanted forest. His first wife was dead, and he had married again to a woman who was always in a bad temper. Nevertheless, he was happy because his first wife had given him two lovely children: a good and brave son named Hansel and a beautiful and clever daughter named Gretel.

One year, the country was hit by a terrible famine. When winter came, the unfortunate woodcutter's larder was empty.

"What is going to become of us? We have no more bread to feed our children. We must find a solution quickly; otherwise, we will die of hunger," said the woodcutter, sadly. Then, his cruel wife had a terrible idea.

"Tomorrow at sunrise, we will take Hansel and Gretel very deep into the enchanted forest and leave them there," she said. "They will never be able to find their way home, and we shall be well rid of them! Then, we shall have two mouths less to feed ..."

"But I couldn't do such a thing! They are my children," cried the woodcutter.

"So you'd rather die of hunger!" his wife retorted harshly.

The poor woodcutter shed a thousand tears, but terrified of this wicked woman's temper, he finally gave in. In the next room, Hansel and Gretel, who were supposed to be asleep, heard their stepmother's cruel words. Little Gretel began to sob.

"Oh, my poor brother, I don't want to be left in that terrible forest. I am so frightened of witches!"

Hansel took his little sister in his arms, hugged her tight, and comforted her.

"Don't be afraid, little sister. Grandfather taught me how to track our way home. We'll get out of it!"

During the night, Hansel got out of bed. Making sure that his father and stepmother were fast asleep, he crept outside, gathered some small white pebbles, then went back to bed without making a sound. Early the next morning, their stepmother opened the children's bedroom door and called them sharply.

"Come on, get up, you lazybones!" she rasped. "We are all going to gather wood in the forest!"

Gretel put on her old apron and tried to blink back her tears. In his pocket, Hansel held on tight to the little pebbles he had gathered. The cruel stepmother was in such a hurry to lose the two children that she ran along the road to the enchanted forest! Hansel followed her, throwing down his precious white pebbles behind him as he went. After a very long walk, the wicked stepmother stopped.

"Lie down beneath that oak tree, and when I have finished working, I will come back and fetch you," she said in a soft, dishonest voice.

Hansel knew that their horrible stepmother was lying and that she would never come back. He lay down under the great oak tree with his little sister. Shivering with cold, they fell asleep. When Hansel and Gretel woke up again, it was night, and sure enough, no one had come to fetch them. An icy wind was blowing, and Gretel began to cry because she was so frightened.

"Be brave, Gretel," said Hansel. "When the moon shines, we will be able to see the pebbles that I threw down on the path. We will find our way back and be home by morning." The two children walked all night through the forest, following the trail of little white pebbles, praying that they would not meet any witches. They arrived home at dawn. The woodcutter was wild with joy to get his children back. He hugged them tight and kissed them. Hansel and Gretel were so happy to be back with their father that they forgot all about being tired and hungry.

But when she saw them, their stepmother gave them a vicious scolding, saying, "Where have you been, you little brats? You disobeyed me! Your father and I have been sick with worry!"

Hansel and Gretel did not answer their stepmother, which only increased her rage. Exhausted, they went to their bedroom and lay down on their beds to rest. The woodcutter's wicked wife waited for a few moments, pushed the bedroom door to make sure the children were asleep, and then turned to her husband.

"Tomorrow morning, we will take them even farther into the enchanted forest," she said. "And this time, Hansel and Gretel will be lost forever. They will never find their way home, and we shall be well rid of them!"

The unhappy woodcutter tried to protest, but his wife started shouting.

"Look around you! We have nothing to eat!" she screamed. "All that's left is one tiny crust of bread. I am not going to die of hunger because of your greedy children. There is no other solution."

The woodcutter shed a thousand tears, but finally gave in to his wife once more. Fortunately, Hansel had overheard their conversation. He tried to go out into the garden to look for pebbles again, but this time, the house door was locked. So he went back to bed and tried to think of another idea. Next day, before the sun rose, the stepmother went to wake the children. She gave each of them a tiny piece of bread and then led them even deeper than before into the enchanted forest.

Since Hansel had no pebbles this time, he had to throw crumbs from his piece of bread onto the path. When night fell, Hansel and Gretel were alone once more, abandoned in the heart of the forest. The moon began to shine, and the two children looked everywhere for the breadcrumbs that were supposed to show them the way home. Alas, the birds had eaten all the crumbs! There was no trace of them! The children wandered for three long days and three long nights, completely lost in the huge forest. Exhausted and starving, Gretel fell to the ground.

"We are lost, and we are going to be eaten by witches," she said, beginning to cry.

Despite his courage, Hansel was also very frightened. Horrible things were said about the witches of the forest that froze his blood with terror. Not knowing what to do, he and Gretel lay down to rest. Next morning, the tuneful song of a robin redbreast awoke the children. Hansel took his little sister by the hand, and they set out again in the hope of finding their way home. They hadn't gone far before they saw smoke coming out of a chimney. There was a house nearby, and someone was at home.

"We are saved! We are saved!" cried the children.

As they approached the house, they saw to their delight that it was made entirely of delicious things to eat. The roof was tiled in chocolate. The chimney was made of nougat. And the walls were built of cake.

Hansel loved nougat, so he climbed onto the roof and ate up part of the chimney. Gretel nibbled a piece of windowsill, which was made of gingerbread. They had never eaten such delicious things! But suddenly, they heard a strange voice from inside the house.

"Nibble-mouse, nibble-mouse, who is nibbling at my house?"

"It's the wind! It's the wind!" the children replied, laughing.

"It sounds more like children to me. And how I love children. So come in and sit down at my table, and I'll serve you a feast fit for a king!"

Hansel and Gretel were still hungry, so they rushed straight into the kitchen. The house door banged shut, and a horrible witch stood before them. Her back was hunched, her teeth were black, her hair was like spiderwebs, and there was a large wart on her ugly nose. The witch caught Hansel by the arm and threw him into a cage. Then, she tied Gretel to the table leg.

"He he! He he!" she cackled. "Now it's my turn for a feast. I'm going to eat you both, but—so that I enjoy you even better—I'll wait until I have fattened you up."

For the first few days, Hansel and Gretel managed not to eat the cakes and pastries that the witch gave them. But after some time, Hansel was so hungry that he threw himself upon all the delicious treats that she had to offer.

After a week, Hansel had become quite plump, and the horrible witch decided he was now fat enough to become her dinner.

"Oh! Scrumptious! This boy promises to be … succulent!" she hissed, looking greedily at her prisoner.

She lit the fire to cook poor Hansel. He was trembling with fear. Then, she untied Gretel, who seemed just as scared as Hansel.

"Climb into that oven, my girl," she said, "and tell me if it is hot enough yet to cook your brother in. He he!"

"But I have never climbed into an oven before, and I don't know how to. Can you lift me up?" asked Gretel, innocently.

"Stupid girl! Look, the oven door is so big that I could get in myself."

Saying this, the cruel witch climbed into the oven. Gretel quickly slammed the door tight. The witch began to burn and screamed horribly. The little girl grabbed the cage key from its hook and rushed to set Hansel free.

"I've thrown the witch into the oven. She is dead, and we are free!" she cried, hugging her brother.

In the witch's living room stood a shining chest. Curious, Hansel and Gretel opened it. Inside, they found magnificent jewels and sacks filled with countless gold pieces. Never was there so much wealth in a single chest!

The children filled their pockets with the treasure and ran off. Outside in the forest, the sun was shining. Hansel and Gretel, who were stronger now, finally found their way home. When they arrived, their father could not hold back his tears, he was so happy. He had been feeling very lonely without his children, and their wicked stepmother was dead!

Gretel untied her apron, and thousands of diamonds fell out. Hansel turned his pockets inside out, and a shower of gold pieces tumbled onto the floor. And so, with all the witch's money, they never knew hunger or poverty again, and for many years afterward, Hansel and Gretel lived happily with their father on the edge of the enchanted forest.

THE END

Tom Thumb

ONCE UPON A TIME, THERE WAS A WOODCUTTER AND his wife who lived in a little house near a forest. They loved each other very much and wanted for nothing. Nevertheless, they were not happy because they had no children. One evening, the wife complained to her husband.

"Ah! If only we could have a child, just one!" said she. "Even a tiny one, no bigger than a thumb! I'd be so happy. We would love him dearly!"

A year later, the woman gave birth to a child. He was perfectly formed but no bigger than a thumb, so the woodcutter and his wife named him Tom Thumb!

The years went by. Tom Thumb had all his parents' love and wanted for nothing. However, he was still just as tiny as ever. But he was so intelligent and clever that he succeeded in everything he undertook.

One day, the woodcutter went out to cut wood in the forest. He was very tired and said with a sigh, "Ah! If only I had someone else to take the cart to the forest instead of me!"

"Father! I can drive the horse if you like," cried Tom Thumb.

"But you are much too small," said his father, laughing. "How can you hold the horse's reins?"

"I don't need reins," said Tom Thumb. "Put me in the horse's ear, and I will guide it by talking to it."

So, the woodcutter put Tom Thumb in the horse's ear and went to sit in the cart. The horse seemed to obey its invisible driver. At the last turning, just before the forest, they came across two men. The men were astonished to hearing a voice calling, "Gee up! That way!"

Curious, they followed the strange cart as it went into the forest and then stopped at the very place where the woodcutter piled up his logs. The child called to his father.

"See, father, you don't need to be six feet tall to drive a horse."

The father got down from the cart, picked up his tiny son, and put him on an ear of corn. When the two men saw the clever little boy, they were struck dumb with astonishment.

"This little lad could make us rich if we took him to the city," one of them murmured.

They went to meet the woodcutter and said to him, "Sell us your little lad. We will treat him well."

"You're crazy! It's out of the question. Even for all the gold in the world, I would never part with my son," replied the woodcutter.

But Tom Thumb had heard the two men's offer, and he climbed up to his father's ear.

"Father, it's an opportunity to make some easy money," he whispered. "And I will be able to travel the country. Don't hesitate—sell me. I'll find my way home, don't worry!"

The woodcutter hesitated a long while, but Tom Thumb was so insistent, he finally gave in. He negotiated a good price with the two men, then he said goodbye to his son.

"Where do you want us to put you?" the men asked him as they set off.

"Oh! Put me on the brim of your hat," replied Tom Thumb. "I can walk around and look at the country."

The man carefully set Tom Thumb on his hat, and all three of them set out. When evening came, Tom Thumb said to the one carrying him, "Put me on the ground, please."

"But you are not disturbing me. Stay there—you are no heavier than a bird dropping," replied the man.

"Yes, but I need to stretch my legs, and I am dizzy from being perched up so high. Hurry up, and let me down," replied Tom Thumb.

Finally, the man put Tom Thumb down beside the road near a field. The little lad ran off between the clods of earth before slipping into a field mouse's hole, which he had seen from the hat brim.

"Good night, gentlemen! Go home without me!" he called at the entrance to the hole, then he burst out laughing.

The two men chased after him and drove a stick into the hole. But it was no use, and furious, they had to let him go. Tom Thumb was delighted to have played such a clever trick on people who had thought they could buy him so easily.

When Tom Thumb came out of his hiding place, he found an empty snail shell, which he made his home. But no sooner had he settled in, than he heard two robbers talking as they walked past.

"How can we break into the parson's house tonight and rob him of all his gold and silver?" said one to the other.

Tom Thumb came out of his shell and offered his help.

"I will be very useful to you. I can just slide between the window bars, and I will pass you everything you want," he said.

When they came to the parsonage, Tom Thumb slid inside and shouted as loud as he could at the two robbers in front of the house.

"Ho ho! Do you want everything that's in here?"

The frightened robbers whispered to him, "Don't shout like that! You'll wake everyone up!"

But Tom Thumb pretended not to hear them and shouted even louder.

"Come near the window, and I will give you everything!"

Alerted by the noise, the maid jumped out of bed and hastened to the door. The two robbers ran off as fast as they could. As for Tom Thumb, he went and hid in the barn. Reassured that there was no one left, the maid went back to bed. Tom Thumb was very proud of his trick, which had sent the robbers fleeing. Smiling, he dreamed that he would soon see his parents again. He nestled in the hay and fell peacefully asleep.

Early the next morning, he was still asleep with clenched fists when the rooster crowed. He was so fast asleep that he did not hear the maid come into the barn to feed the animals.

She took a fork, lifted a clump of hay, and put it into a cow's manger. And in the hay was Tom Thumb, still fast asleep. He woke up in the cow's mouth as she was munching the hay.

"Poor me!" he cried. "I'm being chewed up!"

He understood at once where he was. To avoid being crushed, he slid down into the cow's stomach. But lumps of hay kept coming down into his new room, and there were no windows and no light. Soon, he could neither move nor breathe.

"Get me out of here, I beg you! I'm suffocating!" cried Tom Thumb.

The maid, who was milking the cow, recognized the voice she had heard the night before. She was so frightened that she fell off her stool and upset all the milk. She ran as fast as she could to warn her master.

"Your Reverence! The cow was speaking!" she cried.

"You must be insane!" said the parson.

Curious, the parson went into the stable. No sooner had he set foot in it, but Tom Thumb began shouting again.

"Get me out of here, I beg you! I'm suffocating!"

Terrified, the parson thought the cow was possessed by an evil spirit and ordered her to be killed. Once her throat had been cut, the cow was chopped up. Her stomach, in which Tom Thumb was lodged, was thrown on the compost heap. With great difficulty, the little lad forced his way out and saw daylight again. No sooner had he stuck his head out of the cow's stomach than a hungry wolf snapped him up in one gulp.

Instead of despairing at finding himself swallowed again, Tom Thumb began to speak to the animal inside his stomach.

"Poor wolf! You look as if you're still very hungry! I know where you can have a treat. In that house over there," he said, pointing to his parents' house. "There is a larder full of cakes, bacon, and sausages. If you go through the kitchen drainpipe, no one will see you."

The wolf did not hesitate. As soon as night fell, he ran to Tom Thumb's house, slithered up the pipe, and got into the kitchen. Then, he ate everything in the larder. His belly was so full that it was impossible for him to go back out the same way.

This was just what Tom Thumb had predicted would happen. He began shouting as loud as he could from the wolf's stomach, meanwhile doing a wild dance.

"Stop it!" said the animal. "You'll wake the whole household!"

"Come on! You've enjoyed a feast," said Tom Thumb. "I have the right to enjoy myself, too!"

And Tom Thumb began shouting so loud that, finally, he woke his parents. His father ran in carrying a hatchet, and his mother followed with a scythe.

"Father, I'm in here, in the wolf's belly," shouted Tom Thumb.

"God be praised!" exclaimed his parents happily. "Our dear son has come home!"

His mother put down her scythe for fear of hurting Tom, and his father aimed a fatal blow at the wolf's head. With a knife, they opened the wolf's belly and let their son out.

“We were beside ourselves with worry,” said his father, clasping him to his heart.

“If you only knew what has happened to me,” said Tom Thumb. “I thought it would be easy to get home, but first I had to hide in a field mouse’s hole, then in a snail shell. Then, I found myself in a cow’s stomach and, finally, in the wolf’s belly. But now, I promise I’ll never leave you again,” replied the little lad.

“And we won’t be so stupid as to sell you again,” exclaimed his parents as they hugged him.

So, after all his adventures, Tom Thumb came home at last to live peacefully with his parents, whom he always helped as much as he could.

THE END

Cinderella

ONCE UPON A TIME, IN A GREAT KINGDOM, a gentleman lived happily with his wife—who was sweet and good—and his pretty little daughter. But alas, one day, this gentleman's wife got sick and died. A few years passed, and the gentleman got married again to a lady who was cruel, wicked, and proud. She had two daughters who were as cruel, wicked, and proud as herself. Now, this wicked woman hated her husband's daughter, because the girl's goodness and kindness showed up the stupidity, pride, and laziness of her own two children. The day after her wedding, the stepmother ordered the poor child to do all the hard work of the household.

She had to scour the pots, wash the dishes, and clean the floors. And she scrubbed and polished her stepmother's and her two stepsisters' rooms.

She slept at the top of the house in a dusty old attic. To reach it, she had to climb up a narrow, badly lit staircase. When she had finished her work, the poor child used to sit in the chimney corner among the cinders, where it was warm. That was why they called her Cinderella. She enraged her stepsisters even more, because even in rags with her untidy hair, she was a thousand times more beautiful than these vain creatures, who spent their days looking in the mirror and arranging their hair. Cinderella was very unhappy, but she was so brave that she never complained.

One day, a messenger from the King announced that the Prince was going to hold a grand ball, to which all the young ladies of the kingdom were invited. During the weeks beforehand, Cinderella's stepsisters spent all their time preparing their ball gowns, which gave the poor child even more work, as she was constantly sewing and unpicking, ironing, shortening and lengthening their skirts and bodices.

"I," said the elder stepsister, "will wear my red velvet cloak and my dress with the high collar."

"I," said the other, "will wear my precious tiara and my gown of golden satin."

The two sisters forced Cinderella to be present whenever they tried on their clothes, since they knew she had very good taste.

"Would you like to go to the ball, Cinderella?" asked the younger stepsister.

"Oh! I beg you, don't make fun of me. Look at my hair and my ragged clothes."

"Cinderella is right," said the elder sister. "She would look ridiculous and put us to shame."

Almost anybody would have tried to get revenge for such an insult, but Cinderella, who was not vengeful, took even more trouble to prepare their clothes. At last, the evening itself arrived, and the two sisters left for the ball, dressed in lavishly embroidered gowns glittering with jewels. From the window of her miserable attic, Cinderella watched them go for as long as she could—and then, when the carriage was out of sight, she burst into tears.

From her far-off country, Cinderella's fairy godmother heard her goddaughter crying. With a wave of her magic wand, she arrived in the dusty attic.

"What is the matter, my gentle goddaughter?" she asked.

"Oh! Godmother, I would so love to go to the ball," Cinderella replied, in tears.

"Well, you shall go to the ball, and you will be the most beautiful woman there. Go into the garden, and fetch a pumpkin."

Although she was very surprised to be asked to do this, Cinderella went out and cut a big pumpkin.

With a wave of her magic wand, the fairy turned it into a magnificent golden coach.

"Now, my pretty child, I need a rat and some mice."

Cinderella brought a big rat and some little mice from the mousetrap. With another wave of her magic wand, the fairy turned the mice into fine dappled horses and the big rat into an elegant coachman.

"Go back out into the garden once more. Behind the watering can, you will find two bright green lizards. Bring them to me," said the fairy.

And when Cinderella came back, her fairy godmother turned the reptiles into dapper footmen.

"Now you are ready to go to the ball," said the fairy, admiring the carriage proudly.

"I don't want to abuse your kindness, dear godmother, but dressed as I am, well, I look like a beggar."

"Oh, dear! What am I thinking of?" cried the good fairy, and she waved her wand again and again, until she had turned Cinderella into the most ravishing princess. Her old clothes, full of holes, became a sparkling gold silk gown. Her hair was elegantly styled with curls and intertwined braids. Then, the fairy gave Cinderella a pair of glass slippers that fit the shape of her pretty little feet perfectly. But her fairy godmother had a word of warning for her:

"Take care, Cinderella! There is one thing you must not forget. Before the twelfth stroke of midnight, you must be back at home from the ball—otherwise, your coach will turn back into a pumpkin, your horses back into mice, your coachman back into a rat, your footmen back into lizards, and your magnificent clothes back into rags."

With a grateful heart, the lovely Cinderella promised that she would obey her godmother and be home by the time the clock struck midnight. Then, she stepped gracefully into her carriage, which rolled off into the night toward the palace and the Prince's ball.

When Cinderella entered the ballroom, there was a sudden silence: The violins stopped playing, conversations ceased, and dumbstruck with admiration, everyone gazed at the dazzling beauty of this unknown lady. The Prince himself begged her to sit with him, but then, he found himself unable to utter a single word because he was so enchanted by her. However, eventually, he invited her to dance, and Cinderella did so with such grace that everyone admired her even more. Then, very politely, she went to greet her sisters, who did not recognize her.

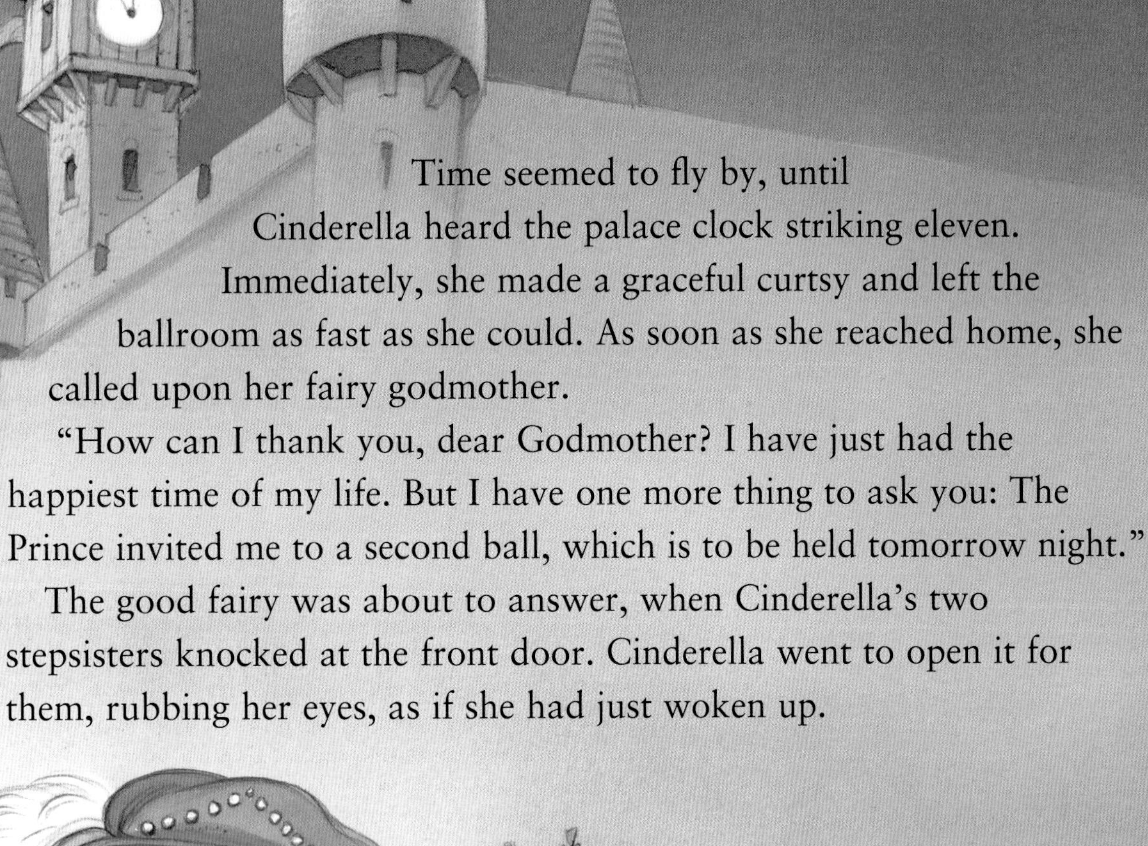

Time seemed to fly by, until Cinderella heard the palace clock striking eleven. Immediately, she made a graceful curtsy and left the ballroom as fast as she could. As soon as she reached home, she called upon her fairy godmother.

"How can I thank you, dear Godmother? I have just had the happiest time of my life. But I have one more thing to ask you: The Prince invited me to a second ball, which is to be held tomorrow night."

The good fairy was about to answer, when Cinderella's two stepsisters knocked at the front door. Cinderella went to open it for them, rubbing her eyes, as if she had just woken up.

"How late you are, sisters!" she said, stretching and yawning.

"We had a wonderful time," said the younger stepsister. "An unknown princess came, who was very pleasant to us. She obviously noticed at once that we are the kind of people to be seen with."

"Nobody knows her name," continued the elder. "We heard that the Prince would give everything he possesses to know who she is."

Cinderella smiled and said, "Please, sister, lend me your old yellow dress, so that tomorrow I can go to the ball to see this beautiful princess."

"What? You go to the ball? Are you mad?" cried one.

"You'd look completely ridiculous! You would make us ashamed," said the other.

And snickering together, the nasty pair went off to bed.

The next evening, Cinderella's fairy godmother waved her magic wand and produced more miracles. She turned a pumpkin into a carriage, mice into horses, a rat into a coachman, and lizards into footmen. And then she turned to look at Cinderella.

"Tonight, you must be even more beautiful than you were yesterday evening," said the fairy. "Instead of curls and braids, you will wear your hair loose. Your dress will be made of the finest silks. As for your shoes, you can wear the same pretty glass slippers as before."

And so, Cinderella left for the ball dressed like a queen.

On the palace steps, the Prince stood waiting impatiently. When he saw Cinderella arriving, he thought he must be dreaming as she was even more beautiful than he remembered. Gently, he took her hand in his, and they began dancing, twirling and spinning, gazing constantly into each other's eyes. Cinderella enjoyed herself so much that she did not hear the clock strike eleven or even eleven-thirty. But on the first stroke of midnight, she tore herself out of the Prince's arms in panic and ran away like a startled deer.

She ran as fast as she could, dashing at full speed down the great palace staircase. In her haste, she lost one of her glass slippers before disappearing into the night. As he tried to catch up with her, the Prince found the slipper on one of the stairs. Gently, he picked it up, touched it to his lips, and then ordered his guards to set out in search of the beautiful unknown princess. But she had vanished completely. Cinderella arrived home out of breath, with no coach, no coachman, no horses, and no footmen, and wearing her old worn clothes. All she had left of the magnificent evening was one small glass slipper.

When her stepsisters came home from the ball, Cinderella pretended to have just woken up. Then, she asked them if they had seen the beautiful princess again.

"She did come," said the elder sister, "but she ran away without even saying goodbye when the clock struck midnight."

"She ran off so fast," continued the younger, "that she lost one of her glass slippers. The Prince picked it up, and he refused to dance or even speak for the rest of the evening. He just sat gazing at the little slipper in his hands."

"He is madly in love with her," continued the eldest, "and in my opinion, he will do everything he can to find her again."

Indeed, the very next morning, a messenger from the King declared that the Prince would marry the girl whose foot fit perfectly into the glass slipper. First, they tried the shoe on princesses, then duchesses, then all the ladies in the kingdom, but none of them had a delicate enough foot. At last, the slipper was brought to the two stepsisters, who also tried in vain to squeeze their feet into it.

"Now it is your turn," said the King's messenger, turning toward Cinderella.

"You are joking," cried the two sisters, laughing unkindly. "Cinderella is just a kitchen maid!"

"I have my orders to try the shoe on all the women in the kingdom," replied the messenger.

He knelt in front of Cinderella and offered the slipper to her. The girl slipped her foot into it, and of course, the shoe fit perfectly. Cinderella took the other glass slipper out of her apron pocket and showed it to her stepsisters, who were astounded.

Then, the fairy godmother arrived, and with a wave of her magic wand, she turned Cinderella's rags into a dress that was even more beautiful than the previous ones. The two cruel sisters recognized the beautiful princess they had seen at the ball, and they fell on their knees and begged her forgiveness. Cinderella hugged them and said she forgave them with all her heart. Cinderella was taken to the palace where the Prince immediately recognized his fair unknown princess. He found her more beautiful than ever—he clasped her in his arms and swore he would love her forever. He married her, and they had many children.

Cinderella, who was as good as she was beautiful, brought her stepsisters to live at the palace, too, and within a year, she married them to two of the lords at court.

THE END

Sleeping Beauty

ONCE UPON A TIME, THERE WAS A KING AND A queen who had no children. This made them very sad. One day, the queen went to bathe in the pond near the castle. The sky was bright and the birds were singing, but the queen was not happy. She sighed.

"Oh, how I'd love to have a child!"

Suddenly, a frog sitting on a lily pad answered her:

"In a year and a day, you will have a child."

Then, the frog disappeared.

After the year had passed, the frog's prediction came true. The queen gave birth to a lovely little girl. The king and queen decided to throw a big christening party and invited the seven fairies of their kingdom to be the child's godmothers. Each fairy was to give the princess a gift, as was the custom at that time. All the important people in the kingdom were also invited to come to the party.

After the christening, all the guests were led into the hall, where a banquet was being given to celebrate the fairy godmothers. Each of their places was laid with sumptuous golden plates and silverware encrusted with diamonds and rubies. Everyone sat down at the huge table. After the banquet, each of the fairies went up to the little princess's cradle to give her a gift.

The first fairy gave her beauty, the second gave her grace, and the third gave her intelligence. The next three gave her the gift of dancing gracefully, singing like a nightingale, and playing all musical instruments wonderfully. But at that moment, a harsh voice shrilled out, making them all shiver. A dark shape entered the room. It was an evil fairy, who the king and queen had not invited. She had not been seen for fifty years. They had thought she was dead or locked up in a tower.

"Ha ha! He he!" she cackled. "You didn't invite me but I have come to bring the princess a gift. One day, she will prick her finger with the spindle on a spinning wheel, and she will die! Ha ha! He he!"

This terrible gift filled the guests with horror. As they stood, speechless and petrified, the youngest of the fairies came forward. She had been hiding behind a tapestry in order to speak last, in case an evil gift was given to the princess. She had not yet spoken, so she said, "King and queen, set your minds at ease. The princess will *not* die. I have no power to undo the old fairy's spell. The princess will prick herself with a spindle, but she will fall asleep for a hundred years—until a handsome prince comes to wake her."

Immediately, the king
passed an edict forbidding
anyone in the kingdom to spin with a
spindle or to possess a spinning wheel.

Time went on, and as the fairies had declared, the princess grew into a young woman endowed with wonderful qualities, and she was loved by everyone in the kingdom.

One day, the king and the queen were called away to their throne room on urgent business. The young princess was left alone and wandered from room to room. Suddenly, she discovered a staircase leading up to the castle keep. She went up the stairs and found herself in a very dark little room, where an old woman was sitting at a spinning wheel.

"What's that?" the princess asked the old woman.

"It's a spinning wheel, my child. It's to spin wool," answered the old woman.

"Can I try it?"

"Of course, my child, every girl should learn to spin."

The princess had barely sat down when she accidentally pricked her finger on the spindle. Immediately, the princess cried out and fainted. The old woman disappeared in a twinkling with an evil cackle.

At the very moment when the princess fainted, every living creature in the castle fell into a deep sleep. The king and queen fell asleep on their thrones, the valets and ladies-in-waiting fell asleep where they stood, as did the guards and soldiers, leaning on their swords and lances. Lucette, the princess's little dog, and all the horses in the stables also fell asleep.

Absolute silence reigned everywhere. Suddenly, thousands of trees, bushes, and brambles sprang up around the castle. The vegetation grew so quickly, that soon, the castle's high towers were almost hidden by it. Not even a mouse could have burrowed through the impenetrable thorny hedge to disturb the sleep of those inside.

A hundred years later, a king's son from a nearby country was hunting near the castle, when he saw the towers peeping out from above the thick tangle of bushes and brambles. He had heard that an ogre lived there or that sorcerers met there at night. But an old peasant told him the story of the sleeping princess and the prince who was to save her.

The prince did not hesitate: He galloped toward the castle. Bushes and brambles came at him, scratching and strangling him. Slashing at them with his sword, he forced his way through. Suddenly, the trees parted on their own, as if by enchantment, and the prince rode up to the castle along a wide path.

A deathly
hush hung
over the castle
courtyard. It was as
if all the inhabitants
of the castle lay in
a deep sleep.

Intrigued, the prince entered the throne room and was astounded to see that the king, the queen, and their subjects were indeed fast asleep. Then, he went through all the rooms in the castle. Finally, he came to the staircase that led to the castle keep and climbed up eagerly. He came into a gilded chamber and discovered the most wonderful sight he had ever seen.

The divinely beautiful princess lay on her bed. Her eyes were closed, and her whole face shone with peace and beauty. The prince knelt down. Trembling, he bent over her and very gently kissed her delicate brow. Then, the princess opened her eyes, looked at him in astonishment, and exclaimed, “Is it you, my prince? You’ve kept me waiting a long time ...”

The prince was thrilled to hear these words and immediately fell in love with the princess. After helping her sit up, he took her in his arms and asked her to marry him. The princess looked straight into his eyes and accepted without hesitation.

Meanwhile, the whole castle awoke from sleep. The king picked up the conversation with the queen where he had left off. Respectfully, the guards and soldiers stood back in attention. The princess's little dog began to bark, and the horses in the stables began to neigh. The princess came down from the castle keep on the arm of her prince and presented him to her parents.

Quickly, the king and queen ordered the prince and princess's wedding to be celebrated throughout the kingdom. The prince and princess lived happily ever after. They had lots of children and often told them the story of Sleeping Beauty.

THE END

Snow White and the Seven Dwarfs

ONCE UPON A TIME, IN THE HEART OF WINTER, IN A faraway kingdom, a queen sat sewing by a window. The window frame was deep-black ebony. As she watched the snowflakes falling, she pricked herself with her needle, and three drops of blood fell onto the snow.

"Ah," said the queen with a sigh, "if only I could have a child with hair as black as ebony, a mouth as red as blood, and skin as white as snow."

Not long after, the queen's wish was granted, and she gave birth to a little girl with hair as black as ebony, a mouth as red as blood, and skin as white as snow. She called her Snow White.

But alas, not long after the child's birth, the queen got sick and died. The king married again. His bride was a very beautiful woman, but she was so proud and jealous that she could not bear to see any woman more beautiful than herself. The new queen had a magic mirror, which she questioned each day:

"Mirror, mirror, on the wall,
Who is the fairest of them all?" she asked it.

And the mirror answered:

"Your Majesty, there's no doubt at all,
You are the fairest of them all!"

The years passed, and Snow White grew up and became more beautiful every day. The queen kept asking her magic mirror who was the most beautiful woman of all. And one day, the mirror answered:

"Your Majesty, you are fair, it's true,
But Snow White is much fairer than you."

The queen knew that the mirror was not lying: Snow White had become more beautiful than she was. Crazy with jealousy, she sent for a hunter and said, "Take Snow White into the forest and kill her. Bring me back her liver and lungs. Then, I will be certain that you have obeyed me and that Snow White is dead!"

The hunter took Snow White into the forest. But when he raised his great knife to kill her, the girl began to cry.

"I beg you, let me live. I will run away into the forest and never come back. The queen will never know," she pleaded.

The hunter took pity on Snow White and let her run away. He caught and killed a young deer in her place and took back its liver and lungs to the queen to prove that he had obeyed her. She had them cooked with salt and ate them.

Meanwhile, the terrified Snow White ran through the forest. She scratched herself on thorns and saw wild beasts jump out in front of her. They brushed against her but did her no harm. Eventually, night began to fall, and Snow White grew very tired.

Suddenly, she saw a little house in a clearing. Since the door was not shut, she went in. Inside, everything was so small that it was like a playhouse. In the middle of the room stood a little table, laid with a pretty white cloth. On the tablecloth, seven little plates were laid, with seven little spoons, seven little knives, seven little forks, and seven little goblets. Along the wall stood a row of seven tiny beds.

Snow White was very hungry and thirsty. She ate a little from each of the seven little plates and drank from each of the seven little goblets. Then, she felt so tired that she wanted to lie down. She tried each of the little beds, one after the other, but none of them were big enough.

Finally, Snow White curled up in the last bed and fell asleep because she was so exhausted.

It was night when the occupants of the little house came home. They were seven dwarfs who worked every day, digging and delving in the mountain to find a little gold and a few precious stones. When they got home, they lit their seven little candles.

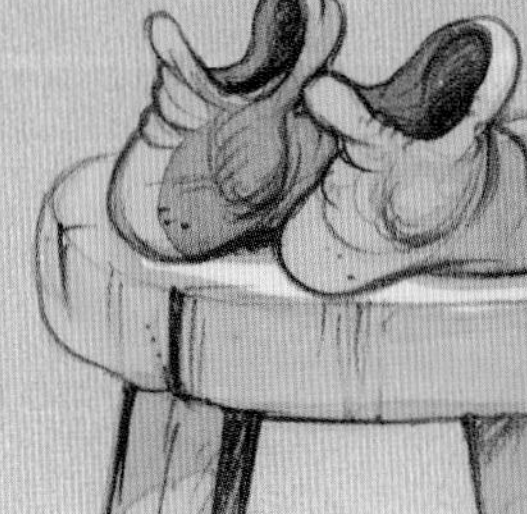

Then, they saw that someone had come into their house while they were working.

"Who's been sitting on my chair?" asked the first.

"Who's been eating from my plate?" asked the second.

"Who's been taking my bread?" asked the third.

"Who's been eating my vegetables?" asked the fourth.

"Who's been using my fork?" asked the fifth.

"Who's been cutting with my knife?" asked the sixth.

"Who's been drinking from my goblet?" asked the seventh.

The first dwarf turned toward his bed and saw that his bedding was rumpled.

"Who's been lying in my bed?" he cried.

Soon, the others ran up, and they all shouted together, "Someone's been lying in my bed, too!"

Then, the seventh dwarf found Snow White fast asleep in his bed. He called his companions, who rushed up and shouted with surprise. They all went to fetch their little candles and stood in a circle around the bed.

"Oh! How beautiful she is!" they cried.

The seven dwarfs did not have the heart to wake Snow White. The seventh dwarf went to sleep with the others and spent an hour in each of their beds.

Morning came, and Snow White woke up. When she saw the seven dwarfs, she was very frightened. But they asked her kindly, "What is your name?"

"My name is Snow White," she replied.

She told them how the queen had tried to kill her, how the hunter had disobeyed, and how she had run all day before she found their little house.

"If you would like to keep house for us," the seven dwarfs said, "and do the cooking, make the beds, and do the washing and mending, you can stay with us. You will never want for anything."

Snow White found the seven dwarfs so friendly that she accepted. So she settled into the little house. Every day, while the seven dwarfs were working down in the mine, she did the housework. She did the washing and looked after everything. When they came home, dinner was always ready. Since she was alone all day, the kind little dwarfs warned her to be very careful.

"Take care, Snow White!" they said. "Don't let anyone in."

Meanwhile, the queen in her palace thought that she was once again the most beautiful woman of all. So she sat down in front of her magic mirror and asked it:

"Mirror, mirror, on the wall,
Who is the fairest of them all?"

But the mirror answered:

"Your Majesty, you are fair, 'tis true,
But over steep mountain fell,
Where the seven dwarfs dwell,
Snow White is much fairer than you!"

Crazy with jealousy, the wicked woman considered for a long time how she could eliminate Snow White forever. Since she was also a witch, she shut herself up in her laboratory. There, she created a terrible poison apple, which was red on one side and green on the other. It was so fine and shiny that no one could resist the urge to take a bite from it.

But the red half was poisoned, while the green half remained harmless.

Then, the wicked queen dressed up to make herself look like a poor old woman. In this disguise, she went to the home of the seven dwarfs. When she came to the house, she knocked on the door and called, "I have fine apples to sell!"

Snow White looked out of the window and replied, "I am not allowed to let anyone in. The seven dwarfs have forbidden me."

"But you can have a look," said the fake apple seller. "Do you see this beautiful apple? It's the only one I have left; I have not managed to sell it. I'll tell you what—let's share it. I'll let you have the best part, the red part, and I'll eat the green part."

When she saw the old woman biting so heartily into her half of the apple, Snow White could not resist. She took the other half—the poisoned half—and ate it. No sooner had she swallowed the first mouthful then she fell down dead on the floor.

Satisfied, the queen gave a cruel cackle and ran away.

When evening came, the seven dwarfs came home and saw Snow White lying on the floor. She was not breathing. They tried everything they could to revive her, but it was all in vain.

The dwarfs realized that she was truly dead. They wept for three whole days. Then, they decided to bury her. But she looked so fresh and lovely that she seemed to be alive still.

"We can't bury her like that in the earth," they said.

So they made her a transparent glass coffin. They laid her in it and decorated the lid with her name in big golden letters. Then, they took it to the top of the mountain and took turns watching over her. Every day, wild animals came with them to weep for the girl.

One fine day, a prince who was riding up the mountain saw Snow White in her coffin. He rode up to her and found her so beautiful that he fell desperately in love.

"Let me take away the coffin," he said to the seven dwarfs. "I'll give you anything you want!"

At first, the dwarfs refused. They told him the whole story of Snow White. Then, they were so moved by the prince's distress, that in the end, they agreed to let him take away their friend.

So the prince ordered his servants to carry off the precious load. They lifted the coffin onto their shoulders and set out. Suddenly, one of them stumbled. Snow White had been roughly shaken, and this dislodged the mouthful of poisoned apple she had eaten. She opened her eyes, lifted the glass coffin lid, and asked, "Where am I?"

The prince told her what had happened and asked her to marry him. Charmed by him and grateful to him for saving her life, Snow White accepted at once. He took her to his castle, where preparations were made for their wedding. The wicked queen was invited, too. Before setting out for the wedding, she asked her mirror:

"Mirror, mirror, on the wall,
Who is the fairest of them all?"

And the mirror answered:

"Your Majesty, you are fair, 'tis true,
But the princess to be is much fairer than you."

Filled with rage and devoured by curiosity, the queen set out for the wedding. When she arrived at the castle she recognized her stepdaughter, who was about to become the prince's bride. The queen was struck dumb with terror, and vowed to mend her evil ways.

As for Snow White, she lived happily ever after with her prince and had many, many children.

THE END

Little Red Riding Hood

ONCE UPON A TIME, THERE WAS A PRETTY LITTLE GIRL named Red Riding Hood. She was called this because one day, her grandmother had given her a beautiful red cloak with a red hood. She was so sweet that she looked like a red poppy, and both winter and summer, she always wore her red cloak. She lived with her parents in a house on the edge of the forest. Little Red Riding Hood was happy and carefree, and spent her time wandering about with her head in the clouds. She was also very good and kind, and she always had a thousand thoughts in her head and a thousand presents for her parents and her dear grandmother.

One day, her grandmother got sick. Little Red Riding Hood's mother made up a basket of good things and said to her daughter, "Your grandmother is ill and can't get out of bed. Take her this cake and this little pot of butter, and spend the rest of the day with her."

Her grandmother lived a few miles away in another village. To get to her house, you had to go through the forest. The way was fraught with danger.

Before she set out, Little Red Riding Hood's mother gave her some final advice.

"Be careful on the road, don't talk to anybody, and be sure to come home before nightfall," she said.

Little Red Riding Hood promised to pay attention and waved her hand merrily. She went on her way feeling cheerful. She trotted along the road, looking at the flowers and birds in the undergrowth.

Grandmother is sure to be delighted if I bring her a pretty bunch of flowers, thought the little girl, forgetting her mother's advice. And while she was putting down her basket to pick some flowers ...

... a big wolf suddenly jumped out from behind a tree! He was hungry and had a wicked look in his eye. But he was also very clever: He knew he had to pretend to be friendly so as not to frighten the little girl. After all, he didn't want his meal to run away! So in his gentlest voice, he spoke to her.

"Where are you going, little girl, all alone in the forest?"

"I am taking a cake with a little pat of butter to my grandmother, who is sick," Little Red Riding Hood politely replied.

As she looked at him with her innocent eyes, he imagined the feast he was soon going to enjoy and was already licking his chops.

The wolf had had nothing to eat for three days, so he was longing to eat her up. In his sweetest voice, he asked her, "Does your grandmother live far away?"

"Yes, her house is on the other side of the forest."

"You know, I'd love to meet your grandmother," said the wolf. "If you like, I'll take this road and you can take that one, and we shall see who gets there first!"

"Alright," replied the little girl, forgetting everything her mother had said.

With no further delay, the wolf, who knew the forest very well, took the shortest road and ran as fast as he could.

Meanwhile, Little Red Riding Hood wandered dreamily along her slow and winding way. And, since the day was fine, she enjoyed herself picking hazelnuts, gathering bunches of flowers, and chasing butterflies.

The wolf did not take long to arrive at grandmother's house. Little Red Riding Hood was far behind! The wolf crept up on tiptoe and knocked on the door. Knock, knock, knock.

"Who's there?" asked the grandmother.

"It's your granddaughter bringing you a cake and a little pat of butter," replied the wolf, imitating Little Red Riding Hood's voice. The poor grandmother didn't notice a thing and called from her bed, "Lift the latch, dear."

The wolf lifted the latch, and the door opened at once. With his claws outstretched, he opened his great mouth, showing his pointed teeth. He flung himself on the grandmother and gobbled her up!

With his belly now as round as a balloon, the wolf licked his whiskers. Then, he shut the door, put on grandmother's nightcap and spectacles, and lay down in the bed to wait for Little Red Riding Hood.

The little girl soon arrived singing, and she knocked on the door. Knock, knock, knock.

"Who's there?" asked the wolf in his big voice.

At first, Little Red Riding Hood was frightened when she heard this voice. But knowing her grandmother had a cold, she replied, "It's your granddaughter bringing you a cake and a little pat of butter."

The wolf called again in a softer voice:

"Lift the latch, dear!" Little Red Riding Hood lifted the latch, and the door opened. When she went up to the bed, the wolf pulled up the blanket to hide himself.

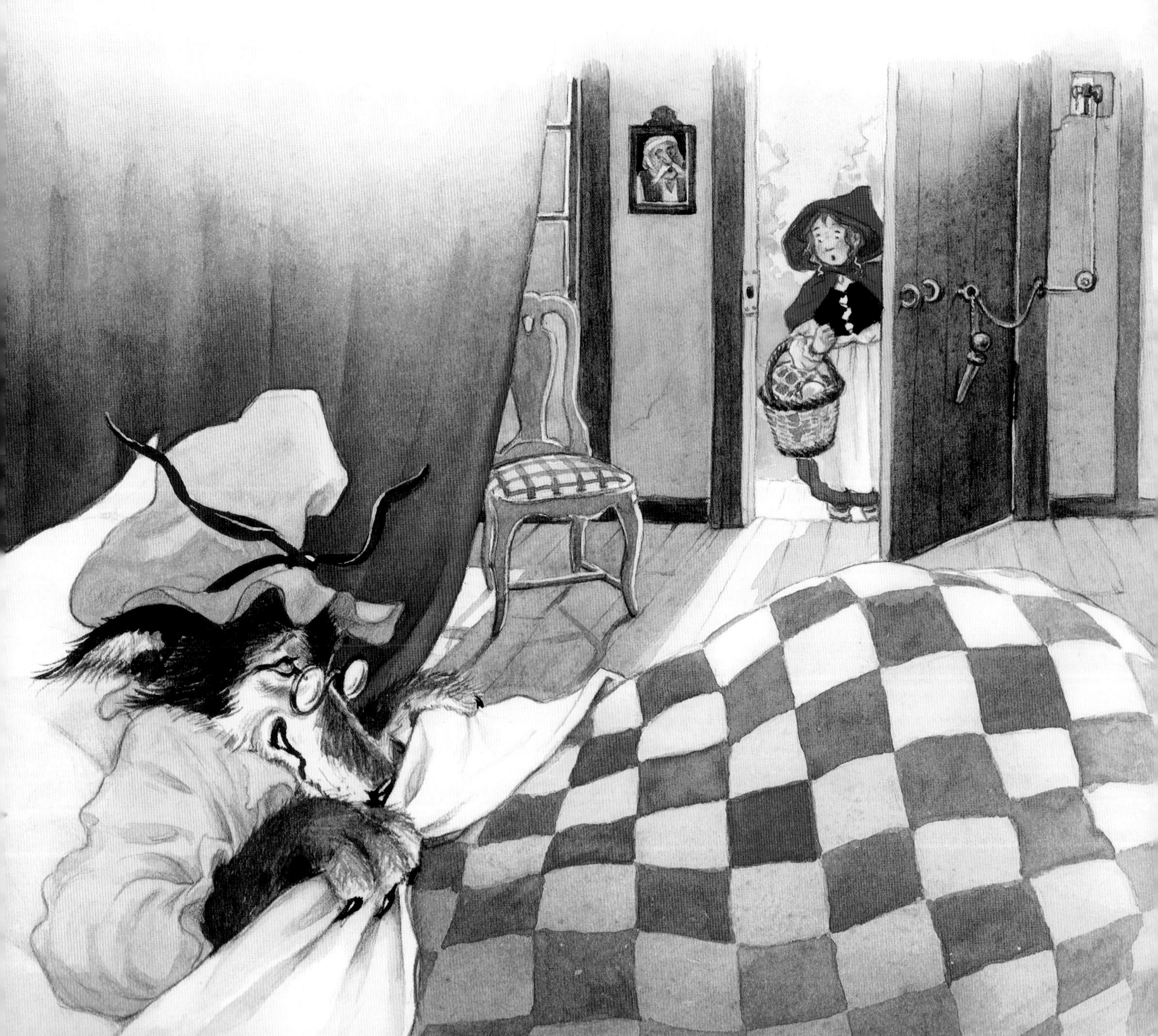

"Come here, my little one," said the wolf.

Little Red Riding Hood went up to the wolf and exclaimed, "Oh, grandmother, what big arms you've got!"

"All the better to hug you with, my child!" the wolf smiled.

"Oh, grandmother, what big eyes you've got!" exclaimed the little girl again.

"All the better to see you with, my child!" said the wolf.

"Oh, grandmother, what big ears you've got!" cried Little Red Riding Hood.

"All the better to hear you with, my child!" replied the wolf.

"Oh, grandmother, what big teeth you've got!" gasped the little girl.

"All the better to eat you up!" roared the wolf, opening his big mouth and baring his huge fangs.

Poor Red Riding Hood didn't have time to realize what was happening. The wolf jumped out and gobbled the little girl up.

He gazed at his big belly, which was full at last. Satisfied, he lay down on the bed, feeling like he needed to rest after all that activity.

He soon fell asleep, and his snoring grew louder and louder.

A passing hunter noticed a strange noise. He wondered how the old lady could snore so loud. Intrigued, he opened the cottage door and found the wolf fast asleep in the old lady's bed. As he lifted his gun to shoot the animal, he realized that the wolf must have eaten the grandmother. Perhaps there was still time to save her!

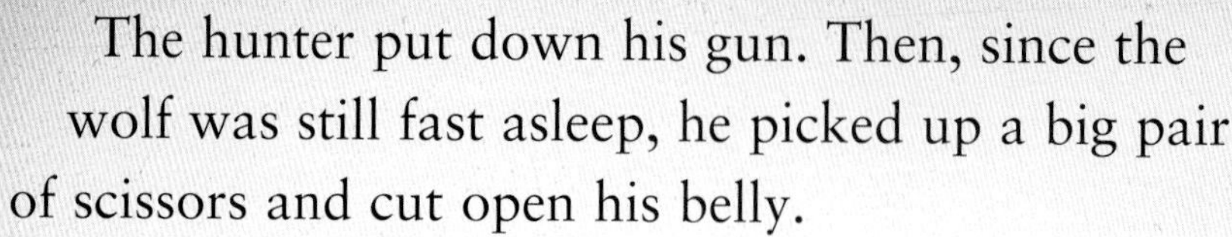

The hunter put down his gun. Then, since the wolf was still fast asleep, he picked up a big pair of scissors and cut open his belly.

Then, he saw Little Red Riding Hood, who popped out, exclaiming, "Oh! How frightened I was! How dark it was in the wolf's belly!"

The grandmother emerged soon after. She was still alive but could barely breathe.

Then, Little Red Riding Hood went to get some big stones, and she and the hunter filled the wolf's belly with them. The grandmother searched in her cupboard and found a needle and thread. She began carefully to sew up the wolf's big belly with the stones inside it.

When the sewing was done, grandmother, the hunter, and Little Red Riding Hood hid behind a tree, not far from the house. Soon, the wolf woke up and felt that his belly was heavy. He got out of bed to go and drink some water from the pond near the house. As the wolf leaned over the water to drink, the weight of the stones dragged him down into it, and he sank straight to the bottom of the pond and drowned.

The wicked wolf was never seen again. The hunter went off, and grandmother ate the cake and the little pat of butter, and she felt much better at once. As for Little Red Riding Hood, she swore that she would never disobey her mother again.

THE END

About the Tales

Fairy tales are folk tales, or fables. In them, all kinds of magical things can happen: Beasts become princes, pumpkins become carriages, and genies appear from lamps. We meet witches, kings and queens, princes and princesses, giants, talking animals, and sometimes even fairy godmothers. Although they can sometimes be frightening, fairy tales can help us to overcome our fears, and they often have things to teach us. Some fairy tales have been passed down from parents to children for centuries by word of mouth. They were not published in books until Jacob and Wilhelm Grimm wrote them down and published them. Other stories were created by authors that we know a lot about—you may even recognize some of the names mentioned in this part of the book.

THE PIED PIPER OF HAMELIN

Jacob and Wilhelm Grimm were famous for collecting and writing down fairy tales that had been passed down from generation to generation. This story—encouraging us to keep our promises, or else!—grew out of a strange, real-life event. No one is sure what really happened, but an ancient plaque in the German town of Hamelin states that on June 26, 1284, a piper in bright clothing led 130 children away from the town, never to be seen again. A street in Hamelin, the *Bungelose Gasse,* or Drumless Lane, was named after the event. To this day, it is forbidden to sing or play an instrument there out of respect for the children who disappeared all those years ago. Different versions of this folk tale were gathered by the Brothers Grimm in 1812. The story was also retold by the poet Robert Browning in 1842 in his poem "The Pied Piper of Hamelin."

HANSEL AND GRETEL

The story “Hansel and Gretel” was first written down by the Brothers Grimm in the early nineteenth century. It was adapted from a tale told to them by a childhood friend, Dortchen Wild, who would later become Wilhelm Grimm’s wife.

There are many different versions of the story around the world. The moral of the tale teaches us that we must be loyal and resourceful, and we should work together and use our courage to overcome our fears.

TOM THUMB

The Brothers Grimm's reworking of this French fairy tale by Charles Perrault describes the adventures of a tiny, clever, and much-loved boy. Tom Thumb decides to go out into the world to prove to himself and his parents that, despite his size, he is capable of taking on life's challenges. His courage and good sense mean that he survives his ordeal—but only by the skin of his teeth. The moral of the story is to be brave, and celebrate your achievements in life, but remember—there's no place like home!

CINDERELLA

Many different cultures around the world have a version of "Cinderella." The earliest-known one comes from China. However, the story we all know today, complete with fairy godmother and pumpkin, dates from the seventeenth century and was written by the French author, Charles Perrault.

One of the most beloved and well-known fairy tales of all time, it has taught generations that true beauty comes from within. The tale also explains how giving but expecting nothing in return receives its just reward.

SLEEPING BEAUTY

Versions of this tale have existed under various names since 1528. It was Charles Perrault's "Sleeping Beauty" that eventually became the most universally recognized title, but "Briar Rose" by the Brothers Grimm is the telling that most resembles the one we know today.

Earlier versions of the story contain events that are unsuitable for children (in the past, fairy tales were intended more for an adult audience), and they continue beyond the marriage of the prince and Beauty into a description of their married life together and their offspring.

SNOW WHITE AND THE SEVEN DWARFS

The Grimm's version of "Snow White and the Seven Dwarfs" was based on an old tale told to them by two sisters, Jeannette and Amalie Hassenpflug, from Cassel, Germany. Walt Disney's famous feature-length cartoon of the story is based on the Grimm's telling. In it, some of the more gruesome aspects of the tale are reinstated. These had been edited out in previous versions intended for children.

"Snow White and the Seven Dwarfs" reminds us of the destructive effects of vanity, and examines the life lessons a young woman must go through before she is mature enough to marry.

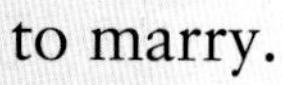

LITTLE RED RIDING HOOD

One of the most popular fairy tales of all time, "Little Red Riding Hood" existed orally before Charles Perrault's version was printed in *Histoires ou Contes du Temps passé* in 1697. It has been the subject of numerous retellings, the more recent of which feature Red Riding Hood being rescued, or escaping, and the grandmother surviving.

The story creates suspense and comedy via the dialogue between Red Riding Hood and the wolf. And it's well-loved even among literary greats: Charles Dickens said if he'd been able to marry Red Riding Hood, he would have known "perfect bliss." The moral that can be drawn from this story is simply not to trust strangers, no matter how courteous and mild-mannered they may at first appear.

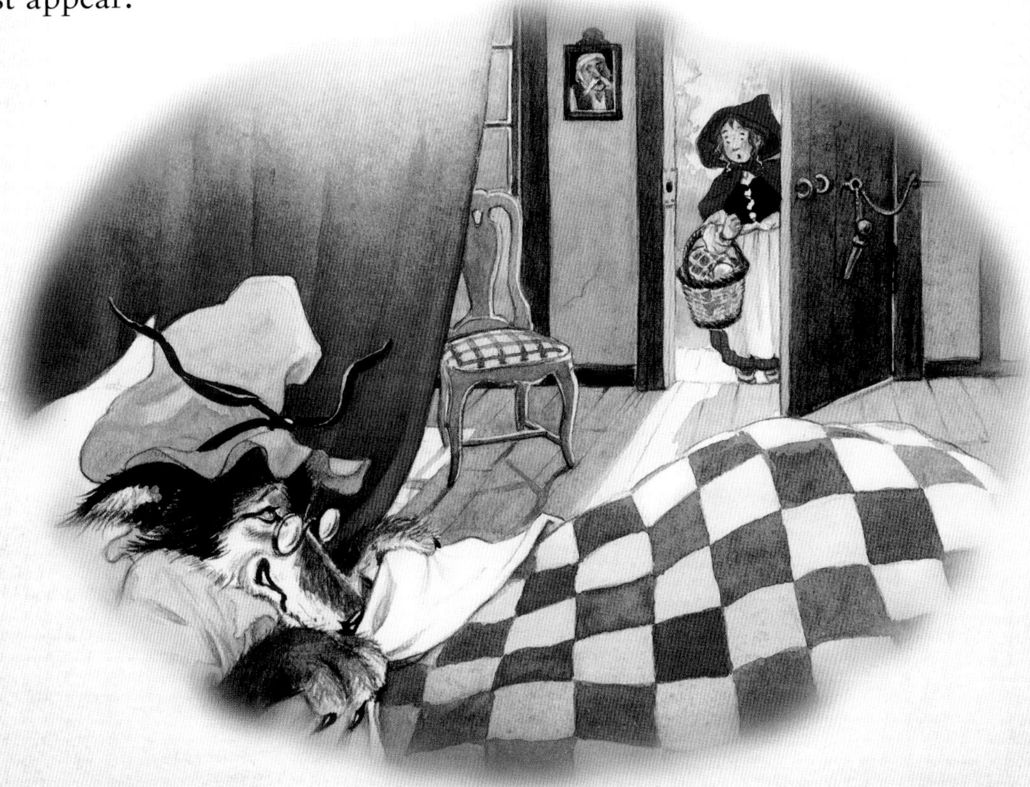